Samuel French Acting Edition

The Convent

by Jessica Dickey

FOR PRODUCTION ENQUIRIES

UNITED STATES AND CANADA
info@concordtheatricals.com
1-866-979-0447

UNITED KINGDOM AND EUROPE
licensing@concordtheatricals.co.uk
020-7054-7200

Each title is subject to availability from Concord Theatricals Corp., depending upon country of performance. Please be aware that *THE CONVENT* may not be licensed by Concord Theatricals Corp. in your territory. Professional and amateur producers should contact the nearest Concord Theatricals Corp. office or licensing partner to verify availability.

be invented, including mechanical, electronic, photocopying, recording, videotaping, or otherwise, without the prior written permission of the publisher. No one shall upload this title(s), or part of this title(s), to any social media websites.

For all enquiries regarding motion picture, television, and other media rights, please contact Concord Theatricals Corp.

MUSIC USE NOTE

Licensees are solely responsible for obtaining formal written permission from copyright owners to use copyrighted music in the performance of this play and are strongly cautioned to do so. If no such permission is obtained by the licensee, then the licensee must use only original music that the licensee owns and controls. Licensees are solely responsible and liable for all music clearances and shall indemnify the copyright owners of the play(s) and their licensing agent, Concord Theatricals Corp., against any costs, expenses, losses and liabilities arising from the use of music by licensees. Please contact the appropriate music licensing authority in your territory for the rights to any incidental music.

IMPORTANT BILLING AND CREDIT REQUIREMENTS

If you have obtained performance rights to this title, please refer to your licensing agreement for important billing and credit requirements.

THE CONVENT was produced by Rising Phoenix Repertory and Weathervane Productions, in association with Rattlestick Playwrights Theater in New York, New York from January to February 2019. The performance was directed by Daniel Talbott, with sets by Raul Abrego, costumes by Tristan Raines, lighting by Joel Moritz, sound design by Erin Bednarz, and projection design by Katherine Freer. The production stage manager was Rachel Gross. The cast was as follows:

MOTHER ABBESS . . . . Wendy Vanden Heuvel

JILL . . . . .Margaret Odette

PATTI . . . . Samantha Soule

WILMA . . . . .Lisa Ramirez

DIMLIN . . . . Annabel Capper

BERTIE . . . . .Amy Berryman

TINA . . . . Brittany Anikka

CHARACTERS

JILL – (early/mid-thirties) A Good Girl who has protected herself by achieving, comes to the convent to escape a marital crisis. A sudden, intense sexual attraction to Patti. In the midst of a massive cracking open of her life and her self. On the verge of major change and deeply conflicted. Which can be exhausting.

MOTHER ABBESS – (late fifties) Wise, truth-telling, powerful, can definitely cut a bitch, runs the convent as her spiritual platform to raise the women's sense of intrinsic divinity. Has her own darkness to carry. (Also plays the **HOMELESS WOMAN**.)

PATTI – (thirty) Sexy, dark, damaged, charismatic, truth-telling, manipulative, but also searching for the light and meaning. Deserves to be saved. A propensity for cutting. And Mother Abbess' daughter.

WILMA – (sixty) A nun. Frank, earthy, very self-possessed. Not what you'd expect. Very present, authentic. A juxtaposition to all the neurosis and drama around her. Possesses the wisdom that comes from a lot of time alone and silence. Came to the convent because she has lost God.

DIMLIN – (late forties/early fifties) From a wealthy British family, but in a way that makes her orphaned, lives off her trust fund. Deeply codependent with Bertie, in love with her but cannot bear the idea of how that might affect her life. Appears perhaps stuffy, even prudish, but really is just sheltered.

BERTIE – (thirties) Younger than Dimlin, sillier, more flirtatious, truly an innocent. Raised in a compound. Has nothing of her own. Throughout the play uncovers her own longing to know love, to know sex, to know more of the world.

TINA – (twenties) Raised in southern California, lost, stoner, psoriasis. Slightly immature, has come to the convent out of a fetish for Renaissance faires. A deep longing for her dead mother and to find her place in the world.

SETTING

Except for the Epilogue, the play takes place in an old convent somewhere in the south of France. Lots of stone and light, a garden. A place where as long as you've got, the Truth has longer.

TIME

The Present.

A NOTE FROM THE PLAYWRIGHT

There were aspects of writing *The Convent* that were true to how I always write a play: I kept the play in a notebook, containing all of my notes and scenes, and indeed the entire first draft. I had spent a great deal of time researching the terrain and subject of the piece, in this case medieval female mystics and convents in France. I wrote a letter to the characters and to the play itself. But nothing else about *The Convent* resembled my previous experience.

The Convent is probably the most collaborative piece I've ever made. Commissioned by Rising Phoenix in 2015, our intent was to produce it in 2016, which due to schedules got pushed to 2017, then pushed again to 2019. By the time we arrived at pre-production in late 2018, I felt safe from the chaotic and pivotal time that the content of *The Convent* was born out of. If *The Convent* were a box and you opened it, a rush of wind would blast your face, carrying howls of grief, guilt, freedom, discovery, femininity, ferocity, and pain. A lot of pain. Um. No thanks. Lived it, learned a lot, grateful for the stable life I've built since.

I knew there was no way I would be able to clearly see the play on my own. If we were going to produce it, I would need strong collaborators. People who were exceptional at their craft, who understood the aims of the play, but most importantly – who loved the jagged, weird edges of the play, who were on board with making something jagged and weird for the audience. I once read that fire ants have the ability to withstand a flood because they take hold of one another and form a kind of raft that can float for up to thirty days. That is what we did to make *The Convent*.

What did that look like in practical terms?

A three-day retreat at Lake Lucille to begin rehearsals. Many sessions of physical improvisations. Great female pop songs circa 1989 at the start of every rehearsal. A lot of hilarious text chains. But mostly? Rewrites. A lot of rewrites. More than I have ever done in a production process. More than was reasonable to ask of our heroic actors and designers and producers and crew (or my mental health!). But they were so lion-hearted and tender toward the play, and they were so like a fire ant raft, we held tight and floated. We even did this joyfully. (The pop songs helped.) This bond was in part due to the nature of the play and its themes – inherent divinity, sensuality, feminism, mysticism, freedom, power, actualization – the play demands that the team show up vulnerable and good-natured, ready to play, ready to connect. And certainly the creative environment to foster such work was entirely due to the fierce, unflinching attentiveness of director Daniel Talbott.

I remember an early preview when I came in with a massive rewrite... I had cut three separate two-handed scenes and embedded only the most important information into a large group scene. I felt sick. I joked with the cast that I had deliberately worn makeup and a kick-ass blazer, so when I looked in the mirror and wanted to cry, I would see looking back at me a professional who had premiered many plays and was in the middle of her body of work. While Daniel took the actors through the changes, I went to each designer and thanked them, as this rewrite meant re-teching a lot of their work. Joel Moritz, our wonderful lighting designer, turned to me and said, "This is exciting. More theatre should be like this." For me that moment was emblematic of the entire experience of *The Convent*.

My hope is that this play is a blueprint for creating a fierce, generous ensemble; a jagged and weird night of theatre that happens to speak to our cultural moment but is more interested in an ancient question that spans a large timescale; and finally, an opportunity to clasp arms with our collaborators and hold tight – we're all we've got.

With great thanks,
Jessica Dickey

Special Thanks to Leah Hamos, Lynn Fimberg, Vern Co, Daniel Talbott, Wendy Vanden Heuval, Addie Johnston Talbott, Rising Phoenix and Snug Harbor, Weathervane, piece by piece, Julie Crosby, Kate Navin, Writ Large, Carol Lee Flinders, Jacqueline Knapp, Catherine Fernandez, Fi Connors, High Point University, the Dickey family, my Montpellier family, and Benoît.

1.

(Lights up on a medieval convent. A large central room, high, cream-colored stone walls and ceiling, full of light. Two women, DIMLIN and BERTIE, are sewing. They themselves are dressed in monastic-looking long brown robes. Outside, birds can be heard. It's a peaceful scene in a faraway time. Until –)

(Suddenly, there is a lot of noise outside as someone struggles to open the very large wooden entrance door.)

(The door flings open and in stumbles JILL, wearing contemporary, casual clothes and lugging her decidedly not monastic-sized travel bags. She has just climbed a biblical amount of stairs and is very winded.)

JILL. Fuck. Me.

DIMLIN. She's exhausted.

BERTIE. She's tired.

DIMLIN. She's tuckered.

BERTIE. She's pooped.

(DIMLIN and BERTIE approach the panting JILL. No matter what their actual age, DIMLIN and BERTIE are like codependent jolly old ladies. Like if Humpty Dumpty had twin sisters, who aren't actually twins or sisters. There's a sing-songy cadence to their quick patter.)

JILL. *(Out of breath.)* Sorry...those stairs...

DIMLIN. Did you arrive with the new group?

BERTIE. Just now?

DIMLIN. Just now?

BERTIE. With the new group?

> (*It's like talking to one person with two heads.*)

JILL. (*Catching her breath.*) Yes.

DIMLIN. Lovely

BERTIE. Lovely.

JILL. (*Trying.*) And you?

DIMLIN. Did we just arrive?

BERTIE. With the new group?

DIMLIN. No.

BERTIE. We've been here –?

DIMLIN. Ten times?

BERTIE. Really?

DIMLIN. This is our tenth.

BERTIE. (*French.*) Dix.

> (*They enjoy a little private laugh about "dix" –*)

DIMLIN. Oh you're learning, are you?

BERTIE. (*Shy and cute.*) Oui.

DIMLIN. Bon travail.

> (**JILL** *just watches all this.* **DIMLIN** *gets back on track.*)

Sorry, I'm Dimlin.

BERTIE. Cora Dimlin.

DIMLIN. People call me Dimlin.

BERTIE. Yeah.

DIMLIN. And this is Bertie.

BERTIE. I'm Bertie.

DIMLIN. Dimlin and Bertie.

BERTIE. Yeah.

JILL. Hi.

DIMLIN. Are you a Taurus?

BERTIE. A Taurus?

DIMLIN. Or a Cancer!

BERTIE. A Cancer?

DIMLIN. The eyes.

BERTIE. The eyes.

DIMLIN. Or a Virgo!

BERTIE. The Virgin!

DIMLIN. The wheat!

BERTIE. The hair!

DIMLIN. Yeah.

BERTIE. Yeah.

JILL. Uh-huh.

DIMLIN. A September baby?

JILL. Yes.

DIMLIN. What was your name?

JILL. Jill.

BERTIE. Jill!

DIMLIN. Oh lovely!

BERTIE. Two "L"s?

JILL. Yup.

DIMLIN. Lovely.

BERTIE. Lovely.

DIMLIN. Lovely.

JILL. ...Lovely.

> (**WILMA** *enters with her bags. She is actually a
> nun, and at this moment, very winded.*)

WILMA. *(Sweaty, wheezing.)* Jesus Mary and Joseph.

DIMLIN. Here we are!

BERTIE. Arrival day!

DIMLIN. What's your name?

WILMA. *(Still winded.)* Sorry that climb was – very humbling.
I'm Wilma.

> (*They shake hands.*)

JILL. Jill.

WILMA. Sorry, I'm a little shaky.

BERTIE. That's just your blood sugar plummeting from the climb.

DIMLIN. You have a few minutes 'til we collect your phones. If you need to make final arrangements. Mother Abbess is very strict.

BERTIE. Very serious.

DIMLIN. No phones.

BERTIE. No tablets.

DIMLIN. No blue light.

BERTIE. Noooooo.

> (**TINA** *wanders in, high as a kite, dragging a duffle bag with a unicorn on it.*)

TINA. This place is incredible. If we do those stairs even once a day, our BUTTS will be medieval too.

DIMLIN. You must be Tina.

TINA. I am!

DIMLIN. *(Referencing a list.)* Jill. Wilma. Tina. Very good.

TINA. *(Pointing to **WILMA**'s nun headgear, her habit.)* I love that. Nice touch. Were we supposed to bring our own nun stuff?

> *(Beat.)*

WILMA. No, I'm – I'm actually a nun.

TINA. *(Wide-eyed.)* You are? Like a real nun? Like Ave Maria?

WILMA. ...?

> (**MOTHER ABBESS** *has entered the hall.*)

MOTHER ABBESS. I remember when I first climbed those stairs.

> *(It's almost like she slipped in when no one was looking, until she speaks and they all turn and see her standing there behind them.)*

I was penniless, lost, exhausted,

but more than that – I was spiritually bankrupt.

No matter what has brought you, what you sacrificed to get here –

No matter your past, your beliefs, if you're rich or broke, thanks to the support of a generous few – you are welcome here.

> *(The air is different now that* **MOTHER ABBESS** *is in the room.)*

DIMLIN. *(Reverently.)* This is the Mother Abbess.

MOTHER ABBESS. Thank you, Dimlin.

(To **ALL**.*)* Welcome to the Convent.

> *(She holds up the Nomen cards.)*

To begin your time here, you will draw a Nomen card, each of a female mystic from the Middle Ages.

Women who, despite grave risk,

heard a voice inside themselves

so strong, so clear, its divinity was undeniable.

Dimlin?

> *(While* **DIMLIN** *says all of the following,* **BERTIE** *collects phones and gives them each a robe. Meanwhile,* **MOTHER ABBESS** *prepares the Nomen cards.)*

DIMLIN. Phones and robes.

The first part of the week will be very structured.

True to a medieval convent, you will work every day –

Share in the cleaning, laundry, the gathering of food.

You will participate in the prayer cycle of the canonical hours –

Prime is at six a.m., Terce is at nine a.m., Sext is at noon, Vespers at six p.m.,

with Complines just before bed at nine p.m., Matins at midnight,

and Lauds at three a.m.

> *(***TINA** *laughs. No one else does.* **TINA** *stops.)*

The second part of the week is less structured, so you can be with yourself and each other.

(The Nomen cards are ready.)

MOTHER ABBESS. It's time to choose your Nomen.

(The women each pick a card. As they get their card, **DIMLIN** *hands them a book with the research on their Nomen.)*

(When **TINA** *draws.)* Julian of Norwich.

(When **WILMA** *draws.)* Hildegard von Bingen.

(When **BERTIE** *draws.)* Clare of Assisi.

(When **DIMLIN** *draws.)* Catherine of Siena.

(When **JILL** *draws.)* Teresa of Ávila.

(The women now have their Nomens.)

The book contains information about your Nomen –
Who was she?
How does she speak to your life?
What is she trying to tell you?
What is she a way for you to tell yourself?
For now, rest from your journey.
We begin tomorrow morning.

(Suddenly from offstage, singing can be heard. The song should be aspirational and sentimental, sappy. **MOTHER ABBESS** *freezes. Her body fills with ice. A brief beat of silence.* **MOTHER ABBESS** *desperately hopes she imagined it.)*

TINA. – Did everyone just hear that?

(Nope. The singing suddenly starts again, coming closer. It's now clear the aspirational tenor of the song is mocking, sinister. It gets closer, louder. **DIMLIN** *and* **MOTHER ABBESS** *look at each other.)*

---

*A license to produce *The Convent* does not include a performance license for any third-party or copyrighted music. Licensees should create an original composition or use music in the public domain. For further information, please see Music Use Note on page 3.

DIMLIN. Oh god.

> (**PATTI** *blasts through the door, belting her sappy, sarcastic, aspirational song at the top of her winded lungs.*)

PATTI. *(Spoken.)* Fuck those fucking stairs.

MOTHER ABBESS. *(Squaring with an old foe.)* Patti...

> (**PATTI** *locks eyes with* **MOTHER ABBESS**. *She holds up her Nomen card – belts out the final cadence, jazz hands and all.*)

> *(Blackout.)*

2.

(The next day. **MOTHER ABBESS** *is working with* **BERTIE.***)*

MOTHER ABBESS. Tell us about your Nomen.

BERTIE. My name is Clare of Assisi. I lived between 1195 and 1253. I escaped an unwanted marriage by joining the Order. I referred to myself as "a little plant."

MOTHER ABBESS. *(To the entire group.)* Yes. Take your Nomen on as part of you, let her speak to your life.
What do I mean when I say *your life?*
What is *your life?*
I can tell you it is not the person your parents raised.
It is not the person you married.
It is not the profession you have chosen.
Or any of the choices you have made so far.
It is not even your body.
It's *Something Else.*

    *(***JILL** *is deeply listening.)*

Think of all of your choices –
as rooms in a house.
As a piece of land, fertile and rich.
Your life moves through those rooms,
it *roams* that land.
And at any moment, *your life* will speak.
Tell us about your Nomen.

JILL. *(Standing.)* My name is Teresa of Ávila.

MOTHER ABBESS. Good.

JILL. *(Rapid and assured.)* Born, 1515, in Ávila, Spain (obviously); died in 1582. I am the patron of bodily illness, headaches, chess (*?!*), lacemakers, lace*workers*, loss, people in need of grace, people ridiculed for their piety, and sickness.

MOTHER ABBESS. That's a very good start, Jill, yes, keep learning about her.

(She turns to the group. A beat.)

Women cannot follow men.

They can *learn* from them, they can *partner* with them, but they cannot *follow* them.

A woman following a man is like a bicycle trying to ride on a train track –

there's great information there, but it's not a match.

You get what I'm saying?

A woman can only follow herself.

Which means a woman must lead herself.

Which means a woman must always strive to be both – the one who is following, and the one who is leading.

The follower in us is relationship focused.

She is a daughter, a mother, a friend.

Things that of course most women are strongly socialized to be.

But the leader – the leader is always in a state of becoming.

She says,

"You are leaving."

Or

"You are a poet."

Or

"Fuck it these boots are worth it."

We could say you are here because a kind of fog has rolled in between you and your leader,

and so your life has become frightening, even hostile, disoriented.

While you are here at the Convent, your Nomen will be your leader,

until you reconnect with your own.

*(***PATTI*** *can't fucking stand it anymore.)*

PATTI. *(Pointing to* **BERTIE**, *a slow clap.)* Oh yeah. Wow. It's amazing to watch, it really is – The performance gets better every year. You have your *minion* demonstrate –

MOTHER ABBESS. Patti.

PATTI. *(Pointing to* **JILL**.*)* And ooooh how do you find someone like her every year?! The tight sphincter Good Girl! The brittle straight As over a vat of RAGE. Your favorite!

MOTHER ABBESS. Enough.

PATTI. *Your Life* IS the choices you've made so far. If choices are like rooms, and *Your Life* just "moves through" them, then the rooms feel a little fucking USED. The rooms feel a little SHIT ON.

MOTHER ABBESS. I SAID ENOUGH. Clear the room.

DIMLIN. Ladies. Garden.

> *(The ladies go to the garden, leaving* **MOTHER ABBESS** *and* **PATTI**. **MOTHER ABBESS** *seethes, all trace of the grace we just saw replaced with ruthless rage.)*

MOTHER ABBESS. We're not doing this.

PATTI. *(Really seeing her.)* Are you fasting or something? You really look like shit.

MOTHER ABBESS. I will call the police, Patti. I swear to God I will.

PATTI. And say what??

MOTHER ABBESS. Whatever I have to. You're trespassing, you are not welcome at this retreat.

PATTI. Now where's the fun in that?

MOTHER ABBESS. I will do it. They'll drag you cuffed and screaming. Don't you dare fuck this up for this group of women.

> *(Beat.)*

PATTI. I'll make you a deal. Are you listening? I'll behave. I will. I'll be so fuckin' quiet you'll almost be SAD.

MOTHER ABBESS. If what.

PATTI. If we talk. *Really talk.* You can say when. But I want to talk.

> *(Beat.)*

MOTHER ABBESS. I say when.

PATTI. Fine.

MOTHER ABBESS. And you never come again.

PATTI. *(Oooh that hurts.)* ...

MOTHER ABBESS. Do we have a deal?

PATTI. Deal.

3.

(Dinner table. Everyone has their head bowed.)

TINA. I want a man with a beard.

Who owns a bakery.

And does community things on the weekend.

Like ecstatic dancing.

I want to not be ashamed of my psoriasis so I can have sex more often.

I want to have sex more often.

I want my mom to come back to life.

I want her to make me Grandma's Toast with cinnamon and sugar cut into four strips.

I want an MBA so I'll be better with money.

I want more money to be better with.

And tits so big I have back problems.

Amen.

Oh! AND! – I want to go back to Ponsie, Ohio and tell Mr. fucking Dannon that he ruined my confidence in math by not giving partial credit and this actually had major impact on the course of my life. And then I want to take a massive SHIT on his desk.

Amen.

PATTI.	**OTHERS.**
Awesome.	*(Awkwardly.)* Amen.

MOTHER ABBESS. Thank you, Tina.

TINA. That felt great.

MOTHER ABBESS. I'm so glad. As we continue to work with this style of "prayer," think about what you would most like to claim for yourself in your life and how you can endow the food you are about to eat with those desires...

*(**TINA** gives a thumbs up.)*

MOTHER ABBESS. Wilma?

WILMA. Oh.

(Everyone bows their head.)

I'm sorry.

I haven't been able to pray.

(Everyone looks up.)

For about a year.

That's – that's why I'm here.

MOTHER ABBESS. *(Gently.)* I see. Then *we'll* pray. You can just say out loud things you might want.

*(**WILMA** gently nods. Everyone bows again.)*

WILMA. I want...

(She slowly looks up. Letting herself dream. And it hurts.)

– A little house with a garden.

Wild fennel, lavender, blackberries.

A deer and her fawn.

My skin warm with sun.

I want...to feel loved.

Guided.

That the world

wants me

in it.

...? ...

I think that's all I can do for now.

MOTHER ABBESS. *(With love.)* Amen.

ALL. Amen.

MOTHER ABBESS. Bon appétit.

(They eat.)

4.

> *(Lauds, the middle of the night.* **MOTHER ABBESS** *leads them into a hall with many white-colored heads of kings. They have an eerie glow in the moonlight. It is very dark.* **MOTHER ABBESS** *holds a chalice. The mood is heightened, there is a sense of danger.)*

JILL. What time is it?

DIMLIN. Three a.m.

WILMA. Lauds.

JILL. What's that?

WILMA. Night prayer.

MOTHER ABBESS. These are the heads of kings. They are an exact replica of the ones in the Museum de Cluny, in Paris. During the French Revolution the people cut off the heads of these statues because they were a symbol of a system that no longer served them. After you drink from this chalice one of the heads of these kings will be replaced by a king in your life; someone you have *throned* and that you hold there, disrupting your connection to yourself.

TINA. What are we doing?

MOTHER ABBESS. You're going to drink from this chalice.

PATTI. Which is filled with a hallucinogenic.

MOTHER ABBESS. A very *mild* hallucinogenic, thank you, Patti – and then you're going to watch these heads of kings turn into someone in your life, a King in your life, who has contributed to your alienation from yourself. The head will speak to you. All you have to do is listen. And tell us what it says.
Dimlin.

> *(She brings the chalice to* **DIMLIN**.*)*

DIMLIN. Me? But – I've gone.

BERTIE. She's gone.

> *(But **MOTHER ABBESS** gestures for **DIMLIN** to step forward.)*

DIMLIN. Bloody hell.

> *(She takes a sip, uneasy. Steps forward.)*

MOTHER ABBESS. Tell us what you see.

DIMLIN. Oh Jesus. It's my mother. You look… I hate that lipstick, Mummy. I've always hated it. It makes you look like a dead person in a coffin. Though your cheeks are holding up remarkably darling, they really are.

MOTHER ABBESS. Tell us what she says.

DIMLIN. *(Listening, uncomfortable.)* She says she's been watching me. Watching her heir.

That I'm getting old.

That I'm a disappointment.

Thank God for my sister who's actually doing something with the family name.

That I was always sullen as a child and terrible when guests were over.

I'd scream things from the top of the stairs like wanker.

She says Cora come home, come home Cora.

Charley Wentworth has been asking about me, Papa thinks it's a good idea.

We've given you long enough.

We can see you, Cora.

Do you think you can hide?

We can see you.

> *(The spell breaks.)*

Oh – …

MOTHER ABBESS. Dimlin?

DIMLIN. She's gone now. It's over.

> *(That was as terrifying and dark as she feared it would be.)* Bloody hell.

> *(She returns to her spot, stares at the ground, disturbed.)*

JILL. Lemme go, I wanna go.

MOTHER ABBESS. Very well.

>(**JILL** *takes a sip of the chalice. She looks at the*
>*heads of kings. Waits. She takes the cup from*
>**MOTHER ABBESS** *and takes another sip.*)

JILL. Come on. I know you're in there. Come on.

>(*She takes the chalice. Chugs.*)

MOTHER ABBESS. Tell us what you see.

JILL. I can't see anything. There's nothing.

>(*She continues to watch the heads of kings.*)

Come on, come on, come on, come on!
Get out here you fucker.
I tried to talk to you.
I tried to say, "Please change. Please change with me."
So say something! Show yourself!
I need you to show yourself.
I need you to show yourself to me.
I need you to talk to me.
Please talk to me.
Or stop me! Stop me from leaving!
You can stop me you know!
Why don't you stop me?

>(*But the king is silent.* **JILL** *slumps down in*
>*front of the king.*)

MOTHER ABBESS. Jill, try to bear the discomfort. Your King
did not come. Maybe that's what you need.

>(**PATTI** *turns to* **MOTHER ABBESS**.)

PATTI. How about you?

MOTHER ABBESS. What?

PATTI. Why don't you do it?
Take a big long drink
And tell us what you see.

>(*But* **MOTHER ABBESS** *is steely-eyed.*)

MOTHER ABBESS. Watch the flame.

> *(Now the women have candles as they file back to bed. **JILL** stays in front of her king.)*

The bright yellow dress that flows upward from the wick.

And the darkness hidden beneath that dress.

And in the core of that darkness, is the brightest ember – different from the flame – more condensed, more potent.

And then beneath that ember is the solid-black wick.

So that always the light and the darkness are entwined.

You are the flame.

And you are the wick.

No matter what is happening – you are always upon yourself.

You need only look in, and whether you see darkness or light, it is all you.

It is all well.

You came to the Convent to see the flame.

You cannot look away.

How powerful it is to stare at something as elemental, and as mysterious, as you.

> *(She exits. Just **PATTI** and **JILL**.)*

PATTI. Are you okay? Sorry. About – the other day. I didn't mean to be a dick. To *you* anyway.

> *(**JILL** gets up. Faces **PATTI**.)*

JILL. Yeah you might be above all this, but some of us need it. So whatever you're doing here, keep that shit to yourself. Okay?

PATTI. So I'm guessing Good Girl isn't gonna work as a nickname.

JILL. No. Cuz I'm not a Good Girl. What even is a Good Girl? Is it, like, is it a star athlete? Cuz if so then hell yes I'm a Good Girl. Is it Ivy League? Cuz right here. Is it Nailed the Bar? Job right outta the gate? At a top firm? Is it a Hot husband (also at a top firm)? Cuz if so, my whole life I've been a Good Girl. And fuck that. I wanna be – I don't know what – Not Good. Cuz I'm not. At all. So fuck you.

PATTI. So what should I call you?

JILL. Jill.

PATTI. Jill. Patti.

> *(They shake. Then **PATTI** suddenly kisses **JILL**'s hand. Starts to leave.)*

JILL. Do you have a Nomen?

PATTI. You know I have a fucking Nomen.

JILL. Okay, who is your Nomen.

PATTI. Mechthild of Magdeburg.

JILL. Never heard of her.

PATTI. She was totally coconuts.

JILL. Really?

PATTI. Like most of the mystics. Absolutely out of her mind. Not that I blame them. If I'd been alive back then I'd have lost my mind too. She wrote steamy romance poems, but instead of a knight and a princess, it was her and God.

JILL. For real?

PATTI. Yup. Sex with God. No shit.
Like a bright wick, englazed
The soul God's finger lit
To give her liberty,
And joy and power and love,
To make her crystal, like
As maybe, to Himself.

JILL. To make her crystal, like
As maybe, to Himself...
Is that – Mechthild?

PATTI. It is.

JILL. So, like back in the Middle Ages, I could've written some God porn and been hailed a mystic?

PATTI. Yup. I mean you would've had to be cool with threat of torture and death.

JILL. Right.

PATTI. Try not to take it too seriously.

JILL. What, my life?

PATTI. All this. Remember it was all just made up by what's-her-name.

JILL. Isn't there some part of you that wants to believe?

PATTI. Believe what?

JILL. That there's a voice inside you – something trying to speak.

PATTI. I would love to believe that. I really would. But I've been coming here for years, and apparently I'm not mystic material.

(*A long stare between them.*)

What are you looking at?

JILL. I'm looking at you.

PATTI. Who's looking – Good Girl Jill? Or Not Good Jill?

JILL. (*Bold.*) Come 'ere.

(**PATTI** *does.* **JILL** *plants a firm kiss right on* **PATTI***'s face.*)

PATTI. (*Through kisses.*) I think I know the answer.

JILL. (*Through kisses.*) Fuck you.

PATTI. Yes please.

(*Lights.*)

5.

(Later that night. **DIMLIN** *sits outside Mother Abbess' room.* **PATTI** *enters.)*

PATTI. Look at you. Guarding her door like a fucking gargoyle.

DIMLIN. Good evening, Patti. Or is it good morning at this point? You're like a feral cat.

PATTI. Do you remember the year I kicked you in the tit? I must've been, what, twenty-one?

DIMLIN. I believe your room is *that* way.

PATTI. And *your* room is *that* way. Yet here we are. At her door. Tell her I'm here.

DIMLIN. Why do you think she posted me at the door? She doesn't want to see you.

PATTI. We made a deal.

DIMLIN. I can't help you.

PATTI. What do you do, Dimlin? When you're not busy being an *heiress* – do you actually DO ANYTHING? Or do you just cluck around Mother Abbess like a cuntless chicken all year long?

DIMLIN. *(You're an asshole.)* I'm an astronaut.

PATTI. Uh-huh.

DIMLIN. What about you, Patti? How's *bartending* working out?

PATTI. Really fuckin' great.

DIMLIN. Clearly.

> *(Beat.)*

It works, you know. The Convent. It works. She built it and it works. But you wouldn't know that, would you? Because you've never really tried. You show up, wreak havoc, but you never actually *try.* And that's how I know.

PATTI. That's how you know what?

DIMLIN. That you're a coward.

A petulant

broken

mean

coward.

PATTI. *(Quiet, intense.)* You don't know shit about me.

DIMLIN. Don't I?

Good night, Patti.

PATTI. Yeah, bonne nuit.

6.

(This scene begins with some jarring physical exercise/exertion using the Nomen names. The women run, jump, scream, it's fun. A nice palate blast heading into this scene.)

MOTHER ABBESS. *(Leading exercises.)* Hildegard, Hildegard, Hildegard, Hildegard, Hildegard.
Catherine, Catherine, Catherine, Catherine, Catherine, Catherine, Catherine, Catherine.
Theresa, Theresa, Theresa, Theresa, Theresa.
Julian, Julian, Julian, Julian, Julian.
RUN!
Convene! Convene!
Hildegard, Hildegard, Hildegard, Hildegard, Hildegard.
Theresa, Theresa, Theresa, Theresa, Theresa.
SHAKE!
Mechthild, Mechthild, Mechthild.

> *(Then she stands next to* **BERTIE**. *Launches us:)*

(To everyone.) Now that you have had time with your Nomen, tell us about her. GO!

BERTIE. Clare of Assisi –

MOTHER ABBESS. My name is –

> **(BERTIE** *says all this like she's sharing something wonderful. She often unconsciously directs it all to* **DIMLIN**.*)*

BERTIE. My name is Clare of Assisi.
I lived between 1195 and 1253.
I was from a really wealthy family, but I left to follow Saint Francis of Assisi.
Actually it's hard to talk about me without talking about him.
It's like we were halves of one whole.

Like those Best Friend necklaces.

Or a clementine.

That doesn't make sense.

Saint Francis was technically my mentor, but we were more like lovers. In faith, not body.

It's kind of a shame, that we couldn't be lovers in our bodies, but...that's the way it was.

So I ran a convent for him, which I found tough at first because I just wanted to pray and starve myself. I was a little wacky about the starvation thing actually.

I wrote a book about how to run a convent.

And I performed miracles! – Like multiplying loaves and curing illness. And there was an army that was going to raid the town of Assisi, but my prayers changed the hearts of the invaders and they left without attacking. I think that's mostly it.

MOTHER ABBESS. How does Clare make you feel, Bertie?

BERTIE. *(Thoughtful.)* Sad.

MOTHER ABBESS. Why is that?

BERTIE. *(True.)* I don't know.

MOTHER ABBESS. Keep talking to her.

> (**BERTIE** *nods.*)
>
> (*The women start running in a circle around* **BERTIE**. *Or they repeat an exercise from top of scene – whatever works from the physical vocabulary to re-energize them for the next layer.*)
>
> (*They stop running. They pant.*)

(To the others.) You don't know what's wrong. You suspect there is a deeper part of yourself waiting to speak. What do you want to know?

JILL. How did you know you weren't making a mistake? When you left your family, the life that was planned for you?

BERTIE. *(Thinks.)* I think I found something bigger. Something that allowed me to be more – me.

JILL. Or *someone.*

BERTIE. Yes.

JILL. You found *someone.*

BERTIE. Yes.

JILL. But what if there is no someone? What if it's just – for
yourself?

> *(She lets out a HAAAAGGGHHH. All the
> women let out a HAAAAGGGHHH.)*

TINA. *(Bad British accent.)* My name is Julian of Norwich!
I'm British (sorry Dimlin).
(Ditching the accent.) I was born in 1342. Ish. And I
was an Anchoress. Which is a badass word that means
that I lived with a cat in a small side room off the
church with only a weird little window to the outside
world.

MOTHER ABBESS. Tell us how you became a mystic, Julian.

TINA. Right. Get this – I got very ill and had a series of
visions. Very intense. And in my visions the cross and
all the walls ran with blood – like A LOT of blood –
and I saw the universe in my palm like a hazelnut.
And God basically "showed me" that sin wasn't real.
Sin was just how we learn about ourselves. And – big
bullet point – that God is a *mother*!!!! And I wrote it all
down. Actually I'm the *first woman* to write a book in
the English language. Ever.

MOTHER ABBESS. Yes! Ladies, your lives are shit! You came
to a cold, old monastery to figure it out. ENGAGE.
What do you want to know?
Wilma.

WILMA. *(Panting.)* Yes.

MOTHER ABBESS. What do you want to know? GO.

WILMA. If God is a mother...

TINA. Yeah.

WILMA. What do you do – if your mother dies?
If you lose your God...?

And you have no idea why?
If you try to talk to your Mother/God
and she's left you alone in your own darkness?

> *(The group is struck by the bottomlessness of* **WILMA***'s question.)*

TINA. – I don't know how to answer that.

MOTHER ABBESS. Just say what's true for you.

TINA. *(Back to* **WILMA**.*)* I don't know. I lost my mom. My God.

WILMA. Me too.

> *(Beat.* **PATTI** *is watching* **MOTHER ABBESS**.*)*

TINA. I try not to think about it.
I miss my mom.
Right in here. Like a well.
I miss hugging her – her soft, saggy breasts, her fleshy back.
She called me bunny.
Julian said, "All shall be well. And all shall be well. And all manner of things shall be well."
Maybe I can imagine my mom saying,
"Oh, bunny.
Everything is going to be fine.
Everything is going to be fine.
And everything you can even think of
Is going to be fine."

> *(***MOTHER ABBESS*** buckles over, in pain but fighting through it, fierce.* **DIMLIN** *notices.)*

DIMLIN. Mother Abbess?

MOTHER ABBESS. I need to rest.

> *(The women start to go.)*

Before you go I want to say something.
There is a Force in this world.
Call it whatever you want.

But She is going to get you.
She is actively seeking you.
Waiting until the panacea of your life
has just enough pressure beneath
that the cracks can be pierced, and she can be HEARD.
And when that moment comes?
It will break open the Lie Of Your Life.
Relationships usually don't survive it.
Safety does not survive it.
You have come to the Convent.
There's nothing here to listen to but you.
Let the socialized layers burn away, down to that dark wick.
Down there, the sooty dark bottom,
She is waiting to speak.
And if you can *bear* to *listen*,
you will step into the *real* wilderness,
the *real* kingdom...
Yourself.

> (*She turns to go.* **PATTI** *tries to go to her. But she has fled.*)

7.

    (**MOTHER ABBESS** *is still gone, so it's like a snow day. They're all together in the garden.*)

JILL. Madonna.

PATTI. I knew you'd fucking say that. Madonna.

JILL. What's wrong with Madonna?

PATTI. Do you have a single original thought in your head?

TINA. I love Madonna.

PATTI. Exactly.

    (**TINA** *sings an off-the-cuff, short refrain from a pop song by a major female artist.**)

JILL. Well who would you say?

PATTI. Me?

JILL. You're so fucking original. Who's your sex symbol from childhood?

DIMLIN. Daryl Hannah.

BERTIE.	**TINA**.
Daryl Hannah?	Oooooh YES.

DIMLIN. An innocence about her. The hair. The mouth.

BERTIE.	**TINA**.
Who's Daryl Hannah?	Yessssssss.

JILL. You know, *Splash.* The mermaid. You know, she's like, in the tank.

    (*She impersonates Daryl Hannah in the tank.*)

DIMLIN. She hasn't seen any movies.

BERTIE. I haven't seen any movies.

DIMLIN. Like literally. None.

BERTIE. No movies.

---

*A license to produce *The Convent* does not include a performance license for any third-party or copyrighted music. Licensees should create an original composition or use music in the public domain. For further information, please see Music Use Note on page 3.

DIMLIN. Zip.

BERTIE. Zilch.

DIMLIN. Zero.

BERTIE. Nada.

DIMLIN. If the movies were a womb, she'd be barren.

JILL. Huh.

DIMLIN. She was raised on a compound.

BERTIE. A compound.

DIMLIN. That's why she hasn't seen any movies.

JILL. A compound?

DIMLIN. A compound. Gunny sack dresses.

BERTIE. Tumbleweed

DIMLIN. Braids. The whole bit.

BERTIE. *(Longing.)* Braids…

PATTI.	**JILL.**
Whoah whoah whoah whoah whoah.	Wow.

WILMA. This explains a lot actually.

BERTIE. I went into foster care when I was eleven.

DIMLIN. After the raid.

BERTIE. There was a raid.

DIMLIN. The police stormed the compound and freed all the women and children. The leader, this cult guy named David Morrow, was arrested for rape and entrapment.

JILL.	**TINA.**
Do you remember him? David Morrow?	Holy fuck.

BERTIE. A little. He had shaggy hair, dark glasses. He once told me I was a lamb.

DIMLIN. Total sicko.

BERTIE. Part of a flock. He never hurt me. I played with the other children. I didn't know.

JILL. Did he ever hurt your mother?

BERTIE. I didn't know my mother.

DIMLIN. She didn't know her mother.

BERTIE. I had an idea who she might be – the sad one, with the hair – but I wasn't sure.

DIMLIN. She never knew.

JILL. You didn't know who your mother was…?

(**BERTIE** *shakes her head.*)

PATTI. The world is fucked. Makes you rethink our current circumstances, doesn't it?

TINA. What do you mean?

JILL. This is hardly being held against our will.

PATTI. Maybe no one is guarding the door but it's still the same old cage, right? What does it say about us?

JILL. Come on. Nuns in the Middle Ages were FREE. A woman who went into a *convent* could learn to READ, she could learn a TRADE –

PATTI. Uh-huh so a NUN could have a little life in a stone prison and not get raped or be made to have a baby (she still had to cook, lest we forget) – Sorry, not buying the liberation through convent line.

WILMA. Hildegard von Bingen changed the lives of the women in her charge. They were educated, they were encouraged not to hurt their flesh. These were big ideas that began a progress we're still pursuing now, millennia later.

PATTI. So what the fuck are we doing here? Contemporary women. Who *are actually free.* Why are we in a convent in the Middle Ages? Huh?

JILL. Because we still hate ourselves. I hate myself. Don't you? I hate my face and my body. I hate my thoughts. I hate my self-hate! I could fuel a SMALL COUNTRY on all this fucking self-hate.

PATTI. So why would being in a convent in the Middle Ages help that? I'll tell you why. *Because women like to be locked up.* We fucking *like it.* And we still want it! We're fucking *terrified* of independence. That's why we do shit like get the big promotion and then get pregnant. Act like the Feisty Fun Girl and then starve ourselves. Or go all the way to PhD in Ivy League schools and then just drive the kids to and from soccer. Contemporary women actually have a lot of great options, and THAT'S what shuts us down. Or makes us shut ourselves down. All these options! And *all our conflicted feelings about it.*

JILL. So what're we supposed to do?

PATTI. I don't fucking know, I hate myself too.

DIMLIN. There *are* predators, you know. Predators who take advantage of women's vulnerability.

PATTI. There are. And fuck them. Fuck them. They're FUCKED.

But women *often* – not always but *often* – take the predator up on his offer. Why? Because they don't believe they can do it without his help. If you're near a predator, get away. Go be whole. Go talk to a fucking therapist and process all your conflicted feelings so you can be an ADULT. You have to give men credit, they get the fuck ON WITH IT. We're very very busy being very very worried about ourselves. And believe me, I'm worried too, because while there is still some serious cultural bullshit out there, I look around and see for the most part women just have to figure out what they fucking want. So we stand a chance of actually making choices in our lives. Our lives stand a chance of being *our lives.*

(*Beat.*)

(**WILMA** *gets up and pours herself a glass of wine.*)

Wilma?

WILMA. (*Pouring.*) Yeah.

JILL. I thought you didn't drink.

WILMA. I didn't.

(*She drinks.*)

Hm. Not bad.

TINA. I like a flaccid penis.

JILL. What?

TINA. The penis when it's flaccid. It's like a little baby bird. I just wanna kiss it and like, squish it. All the folds and the weird little weepy EYE. A hard penis is so. There's all this pressure to *do something about it*. But a squishy penis you can just lay together in the afternoon sun and think your thoughts, play lightly with Mr. Squishy and just – *be*.

JILL. I'm beginning to really like you.

TINA. Thank you.

> *(Beat.)*

> *(**TINA** performs the entire song [from earlier] for the group.* It should feel fun, feminist, even flirtatious. Eventually **JILL** joins in, then everyone. The moment should feel spontaneous and fun, but also possess a sweetness, like you can picture each of them as teenage girls just living for this song. The whole group rocks out together.)*

(Really on a roll now.) My mom dated this guy that worked at a Renaissance faire. She'd been diagnosed but she was still really strong. He'd take us around the faire, in character you know? Everybody loved Renlin the Fruitseller.

One night my mom said, "Tina, three things:

Don't waste your time on a cheap man. Don't judge him for being *poor*, but if he's *cheap*? – Get Out. Two – if he's over thirty-five and has no idea what he's doing with his life, he's never going to know and it's a compulsion in his personality – so Get Out. And three – if he doesn't go down on you very often? – It

---

*A license to produce *The Convent* does not include a performance license for any third-party or copyrighted music. Licensees should create an original composition or use music in the public domain. For further information, please see Music Use Note on page 3.

means he doesn't like it, and if he doesn't like it? – Then on some level he doesn't like *you*. So Get Out."

(*Everyone contemplates this.*)

JILL. Did Teresa of Ávila hate herself? Did Julian of Whatever –

TINA. Norwich.

JILL. Norwich hate herself? Maybe. But they still somehow – what? – they *heard it.*

DIMLIN. They heard what?

JILL. I don't know, something powerful – it spoke directly to them – right into their ear – so clearly that it pierced that self-hate – and we're hearing them still. Hundreds of years later.

BERTIE. Maybe that's why Clare starved herself. She was testing her will. Seeing what she was really made of.

DIMLIN. Catherine of Siena was a bloody BEAST for God. She was a fierce force for peace, appealing to warring families, city-states throughout Italy, between popes and political factions. A lot of crazy nonsense happened in the Italian church from 1347 to 1380, and she was IN IT. Maybe men have conquered continents. Scaled mountains. But Catherine of Siena scaled the highest Everest possible. The one on the inside. And that is bloody worth doing. Even if she should've had more cake now and then.

BERTIE, JILL, TINA & WILMA. (*A victory cry.*) Caaaaake.

TINA. Wilma, if you've been a nun, does that mean you've, like, never had sex?!

WILMA. No.

TINA. Never?!

WILMA. No.

TINA. (*Makes robot sounds.*) Meep morp merrrhhhhh.

WILMA. Is that so hard to imagine? Some women feel virginity is more natural than anything else.

PATTI. You've never had sex with a *man* or you've never had sex with a *woman*?

(**BERTIE** *suddenly burps out a giggle/snort.*)

BERTIE. Can you have sex with a woman??

DIMLIN. Oh naughty.

BERTIE. Naughty.

DIMLIN. Tres tres naughty.

BERTIE. Tres tres.

(*Beat.*)

But can you?

(*Beat.*)

PATTI. (*Very pointed.*) YES, Bertie. *You.* Can Have *Sex.* With a *Woman.*

(*Beat.*)

WILMA. It's not a new idea. The idea that sex mutes God. It's not for everyone, that's why it's a Calling. But it was right for me. So I could hear God.

PATTI. Unless you lose that too.

WILMA. (*Oooh that's some truth.*) Yes.

BERTIE. (*Can't shake this.*) How? How do you have sex with a woman?

DIMLIN. (*Scared.*) Bertie.

BERTIE. What?

DIMLIN. Naughty.

BERTIE. How?

PATTI. Want me to tell you?

(**BERTIE** *nods. Intense, intimate:*)

You feel everything.

You feel her.

You touch her.

You touch everything.

Everything gives. Everything is soft. Even her hip bones are soft.

You take your time.

You let go of any sense of that old shape, that old *crest.*

Sex with a woman isn't the old *wave*. Rise and then crash.
It's many many waves. Over and over.
And you can go down to the bottom and come back up.
As many times as you like. As she likes.
That horizon is not flat. It's a curve. It's many curves.
There's nothing you need to *do*.
You just open your hands and your mouth and let her *do it on you.*
Let her lead.
But be right there with her. So she won't look down.
As long as she feels you right there, she'll fly.

> *(The air in the room has changed.* **BERTIE** *is weeping without realizing it.)*

DIMLIN. Bertie.

> *(***BERTIE*** *pulls away, shaken, then runs out of the room.)*

Bertie.

> *(She gets up to run out after* **BERTIE**. *Turns and sees everyone watching her, so she exits a different direction.)*

TINA. *(Quietly.)* Fuck me that was intense.
Intense intense intense.

> *(***TINA*** *leaves to masturbate. Or eat. Or both.)*

> *(***WILMA*** *watches.)*

> *(***JILL*** *kisses* **PATTI**. *Kissing, tongues, hands. They exit.)*

> *(***WILMA*** *is left onstage sipping her wine, contemplating the sunset.)*

> *(Blackout.)*

8.

*(Dinner table. Heads bowed. **JILL** and **MOTHER ABBESS** are mid-fight.)*

JILL. All I can think about is what I DON'T want.

MOTHER ABBESS. Okay.

JILL. Like I DON'T want to wax my vagina. Like *ever*. It hurts soooo much and it gets infected and it it it just hurts.

I don't want to skip dessert.

I don't want...to be so confused... I mean what are we even doing?

MOTHER ABBESS. Instead of asking the divine to "bless" your food, you are endowing the food with the desires of your heart. And then by eating that food, you give yourself those desires.

JILL. Am I in trouble?

MOTHER ABBESS. Why would you be in trouble?

JILL. I don't know.

MOTHER ABBESS. Maybe for having sex in the sacristy.

Or for having sex in the wine cellar.

Or my office.

Try again.

JILL. ...

I *do* want to punch women who count calories in the head.

I want to take the way my husband says the word Wife – with a capital W – and I want to shove it in his mouth.

I want nine lives.

I want to kiss everything with a heartbeat.

I want to sit on a stubbled man's face and suffocate him as I come to a full moon.

I want to be good at high heels.

I want to have buff fucking arms.

I want a pet grizzly bear that walks next to me.

I want to say, "SOME OF US HAVE BEEN JUGGLING THERAPY AND OUR JOBS FOR YEARS SO THIS 'ONE THING AT A TIME' THING IS REALLY PRETTY LAME."

I want to say, "YOU ARE CHEAP."

I want to say, "YOU'VE ACTUALLY NEVER APOLOGIZED FOR A SINGLE THING,

AND YOU NEVER *GROW*."

I want to say I'm sorry.

I'm sorry that I changed.

I'm sorry that you didn't change enough.

I'm sorry I didn't realize I wasn't happy.

That I didn't reach an ultimatum and give it to you.

I'm sorry that all of those pictures and songs and memories and camping trips and inside jokes are going to hurt. For a really really long time.

I'm sorry that despite my best intentions, I'm going to keep hurting you.

That everything I do is going to hurt you over and over and over again.

I'm sorry that we'll never really speak again.

We'll speak, we'll see each other, ask how we are, but the old you, the old me, the people who loved each other, we will never see each other again.

I'm sorry I need more. And I do. I need more.

I'm sorry there is no possible way, to say I'm sorry for that.

But I want to.

I want to say I'm sorry over and over again for the rest of my life.

I don't want to be your wife.

I don't want to be anyone's wife.

I want to be *my* wife.

I want to be my own.

I want,

someday,
I want you to understand.
To recognize the ways I tried to keep you near.
I want you to love me for trying.
And forgive me for failing.
And respect me for leaving.
For being brave enough to do the thing that I believe
someday we'll both be glad I did.
And then I want you to be happy.
And I want to be happy too.
Amen.

ALL. Amen.

MOTHER ABBESS. Good for you, Jill. Yes. Amen.

ALL. Amen.

> *(The group starts to say "Amen," but* **BERTIE**
> *keeps praying.)*

BERTIE. *(Lost in her thoughts.)* I want a pair of red shoes
   that are sexy but comfy enough for long walks.
   I want box seats at the opera.
   I want to see a UFO.
   I want to feel like a rose, fresh in the morning dew.
   I want to feel the warm sun peel my petals open, slowly,
   oh so gently,
   like warm feminine hands,
   letting the warm light work its way down into the
   darkness of my undiscovered crevices,
   where there is nectar.

> *(A few people look up. What's happening?*
> **BERTIE** *remains deeply entranced.)*

Sweet, sticky nectar, clinging patiently to a firm stamen.
And then sun will creep into that darkness,
like a tongue of light, the gentlest fire,
and my fragrance will dispel, like a sigh,
and the entire flower of my being will open,

will gasp open,
grabbing hold of that tongue that light with a fierce
hunger and pull it – down onto my wet wet
craaaaahhhhhh I want to have sex.
I want to have sex. Dimlin?

*(Everyone looks up now. **DIMLIN** is frozen.)*

DIMLIN. What?

BERTIE. I want you to touch me, why can't we touch each
other?

DIMLIN. Bertie.

BERTIE. Why can't we love each other? I want you to love
me. Make love to me Dimlin.

DIMLIN. *(Shocked, mortified.)* Bertie! – I – I can't –

BERTIE. Please Dimlin. I want to make love.

DIMLIN. *(Getting up.)* No. Nonononono.

BERTIE. Dimlin please!

DIMLIN. No! No!

*(She runs out. No one knows what to say.
Beat. **BERTIE** suddenly returns to the table,
sits. Beat.)*

MOTHER ABBESS. I suppose this is as good a moment as any
to hear a mandatory word from our sponsor.

(She clearly dreads this every year.)

Good Christian Women would like to welcome you to
this contemplative retreat. *Good Christian Women...
Because women are the cornerstone of faith.*
Bon app.

9.

(That night. Mother Abbess' door. **DIMLIN** *is guarding it.* **PATTI** *enters.)*

PATTI. *(Almost gently.)* Hello again.

DIMLIN. She doesn't want to speak with you.

>*(Beat.)*

PATTI. You know what I keep thinking this year? We're getting old. You're getting old. I'm getting old. *She's getting old.* We're all – getting old.

>*(Beat.)*

DIMLIN. *(So still it's like her clothes are keeping her molecules together.)* Every single thing takes two hours. Have you noticed that?

Dinner has to be gathered and washed and cut and prepped, the wood has to be chopped, the fire has to be built and tended, the meal slow-cooked.

The dishes have to be washed by hand with a bar of soap that you already used on your laundry that morning with a rock.

There's no time to sit and think about your shitty self.

There's only the day's tasks, and because they take so long there's only about *four.*

You think you're an interesting person? Well good for you. Have at it.

I *know* I'm not an interesting person.

I've read a few good books and can identify edible forest mushrooms and that's about it.

But here at the Convent? – I needn't be more.

I think it must be what an animal feels.

This quiet plodding from this to that, and I love it.

For me it is peace.

Or at least...

PATTI. It *was.* Yeah – this year seems to be going a bit differently.

DIMLIN. …

PATTI. We're not so different, you know. We both want something very much. And our whole life is constructed around not having it.

DIMLIN. Go to bed.

PATTI. I'm fighting for what I want.
You should try it. Before it's too late.

> *(She starts to leave, and then suddenly:)*

DIMLIN. Patti?

> *(**PATTI** turns back.)*

(A gift.) She went to smoke. In the courtyard. You might find her there.

10.

(Meanwhile, in the courtyard, **JILL** *enters.* **MOTHER ABBESS** *is smoking in the corner.)*

MOTHER ABBESS. *(From the dark.)* Can't sleep?

JILL. No.

MOTHER ABBESS. Me either. Want one?

JILL. Sure.

(They smoke.)

MOTHER ABBESS. You have the mark.

JILL. The mark? What's the mark?

MOTHER ABBESS. It has to do with destruction. And freedom. Not everyone has it, but you do.

JILL. How do you know?

MOTHER ABBESS. Because I have it too.

(Beat.)

I left my child.

She was four. We were in Providence. My husband *[Pronounced the French way.]* Jean was finishing his postdoc. He was excited to have a child. I thought I would get there. One night I'd gone to bed early with a very bad headache, when I suddenly had this intense feeling that I needed air. So I went out into the yard and there, at the edge of my property, was a row of statues.

(The women of the Convent wear masks and robes all of white, like marble. They stand in various poses like medieval statues – a row of statue women caught mid-gesture. **MOTHER ABBESS** *and* **JILL** *walk among them.)*

They were women. Marble breasts beneath marble gauze. Hips and thighs. I could see their lips, their white eyes, their hair frozen in a stone curl. They stood there – almost like they were mid-gesture – as if something in them had been cut short – they had been in the middle of an idea, or thinking of a poem, or directing a meal – and suddenly – it was done.

I had no idea what was happening. Something was cracking open. I stood among them, my hands outstretched, and I knew. I knew I would leave.

JILL. But didn't you love your daughter?

MOTHER ABBESS. I did. But with her came an unbearable sadness. A suffocation that I couldn't endure and stay alive. I wandered around Europe, working on farms, staying at ashrams and monasteries. I didn't know what the fuck I was doing. I thought I might die. I was searching for a sense that I possessed divinity. Sovereignty.

JILL. Sovereignty…

MOTHER ABBESS. I never liked church. I hated being told what to say, I hated being talked to through the words "he" and "mankind." I felt like spirituality was this little peephole I was allowed to look through, into this room that other people got to be in. But spirituality is exactly what I was seeking. Sovereignty. True sovereignty.

(The statues fade.)

JILL. Do you ever see your daughter now?

MOTHER ABBESS. All the time.

JILL. All the time? Oh, like she's your King?

MOTHER ABBESS. Well she is that, she is my King. But she actually comes here, to the Convent. She –

*(**PATTI** enters.)*

PATTI. Here you are.

JILL. Hi! We can't sleep.

PATTI. That's funny. Neither can I.

JILL. *(Sweet.)* Come here. Smoke with us.

PATTI. I don't want to interrupt if there's a spiritual epiphany happening.

JILL. Shut up and come here. You can share mine.

(**PATTI** *delicately enters, takes a drag off* **JILL***'s cig. Then* **MOTHER ABBESS** *holds out the pack.*)

MOTHER ABBESS. Here. Have your own.

PATTI. –? Okay.

(**JILL**, **PATTI**, *and* **MOTHER ABBESS** *all stand there smoking. It kind of works. There's a peace.*)

JILL. It's a beautiful night.

MOTHER ABBESS. It is.

JILL. Where do you live? When you're not here?

MOTHER ABBESS. Paris.

(**PATTI** *doesn't know any of this. And* **MOTHER ABBESS** *knows it.*)

JILL. Paris. That's cool. Do you work there, or is this, like, your main jam?

MOTHER ABBESS. Uhhhm.

(*A beat while she debates whether to continue.*)

JILL. Sorry is that private?

MOTHER ABBESS. I don't –. I don't usually...

(*Beat.*)

PATTI. (*A save? A competition? An offering? All the above?*) Paris is a beautiful city.

MOTHER ABBESS. It is.

(*Beat.*)

PATTI. (*Gently pressing forward.*) I built a cabin.

(*It's like since* **JILL** *is there,* **MOTHER ABBESS** *and* **PATTI** *can actually talk a little. It's delicate, a little nervy, but it's a start. It feels good.*)

JILL. Really?

PATTI. Well, it's more like a shack. A poetry shack.

JILL. A poetry shack (you're so rad). Where?

PATTI. (*Half-eyed toward* **MOTHER ABBESS**.) This plot of land, outside the city. Days off I can close the bar at three a.m. and can get there by dawn. Make coffee and get to work.

JILL. I wouldn't have the first fuckin' idea how to build a cabin.

PATTI. You'd be surprised. It's not much, it's super small, and not very weatherproof. But there are rugs on the floor, a small wood-burning stove, bedding. In the morning you sit outside and watch the mist on the lake.

MOTHER ABBESS. Sounds beautiful.

PATTI. It is.

> (*Beat. Better quit while they're ahead –*)

MOTHER ABBESS. (*Finishing her cigarette.*) I should get some sleep.

PATTI. Have another.

MOTHER ABBESS. Not tonight.

PATTI. Come on, just one more.

> (*Beat.*)

MOTHER ABBESS. Good night.

JILL. 'Night, Mother Abbess.

MOTHER ABBESS. Good night, Jill.

> (*She starts to go.*)

PATTI. It's funny. Choosing to be called *Mother*.

> (*Beat.*)

MOTHER ABBESS. Good night, Patti.

PATTI. I dare you. I dare you to have another.

JILL. (*No idea what they're entering.*) Patti.

PATTI. I dare you.

MOTHER ABBESS. Let's just...

PATTI. Let's just what?

MOTHER ABBESS. I'm not your enemy.

PATTI. What are you then?

MOTHER ABBESS. Why? Why come if you hate it so much?

PATTI. You know why.

MOTHER ABBESS. I keep waiting for you to figure out who you are.

PATTI. Oh like you know who I am.

JILL. Should I –? – go?

PATTI. No stay, I want you to stay, please continue, *MOTHER*.

MOTHER ABBESS. All right, enough.

PATTI. No come on. Who am I? Who am I, *Joan*? Joan Rubenstein of Malvern, Pennsylvania. There. That's who you are. So who am I?

MOTHER ABBESS. Stop this.

PATTI. Come on, this'll be fun. Say it. Say who I am. Say it. Say it. Say it. Say it. SAY IT. SAY IT.

MOTHER ABBESS. You're my daughter.

PATTI. Sorry, I couldn't catch that.

MOTHER ABBESS. You're my daughter.

> *(Beat.)*

JILL. Wait. What?

MOTHER ABBESS. Patti is my daughter, Jill.

JILL. *(Did not see that coming; gently.)* Oh. Oh wow.

MOTHER ABBESS. I'm sorry you're in the middle of – It was my end of the deal with her father, Jean. I think he honestly hoped we'd eventually – connect. But it probably would have been better if I'd disappeared. Then she could make up a legend about me. Like one of those canonized mystics. She could weed out the oddities, the unsettling inconsistencies, and just keep what supports her image of me. Whatever image she wanted to keep. Instead, we look at each other and only see the truth.

> *(JILL looks back and forth between* **MOTHER ABBESS** *and* **PATTI**.*)*

JILL. What truth is that?

PATTI. She doesn't want to be a mother.

> *(MOTHER ABBESS starts to leave.)*

PATTI. Yeah good, go, we're gonna do something a lot more fun than this anyway. It's called A GOOD FUCK. Try it sometime.

> (**MOTHER ABBESS** *suddenly wheels around, ferocious.*)

MOTHER ABBESS. You're fucking right! I don't want to be a mother! I don't want to be a mother! And you know what?? – That is my MOTHERFUCKING RIGHT.

PATTI. Your right?!?! Can you even hear yourself?! You disgust me!

MOTHER ABBESS. GOOD! BE DISGUSTED! It was a terrible decision, it almost killed me, I almost *died*!

PATTI. Well maybe that should tell you something! It was the WRONG DECISION and your life has been a LIE ever since!

> (*It's like watching wolves.*)

MOTHER ABBESS. Patti, I've got bad news, and Jill you may as well hear this too: There is no way to be true to yourself without blood. To choose yourself means to let someone else break. That's the way it is. I'm sorry it was you, Patti. I see that it was. But the sooner you look in the fucking mirror and figure out who you are the sooner your life will actually begin. And you won't do that 'til you let go of me. And you DESERVE THAT. Please hear me – you deserve life. You deserve love and beauty and happiness.

PATTI. NO you don't get to do that. You don't get to DITCH ME and then look at me and tell me I'm worthy of love.

MOTHER ABBESS. The truth comes to us. Terrible and swift. So we make choices. We do our best. And there are costs. Yes. But only *we know*. Only *we* will ever know the cost of *not listening*.

My advice to you, Jill? – If you're going, then go. Don't go halfway.

PATTI. What would you do if I burned this place down? Lit a match to your precious Convent and let it burn to the fucking ground?

MOTHER ABBESS. I would build another. And then another. And then another.

> *(Beat.)*

PATTI. *(Simply.)* That's how you're supposed to feel about me.

> *(Beat.)*

MOTHER ABBESS. Then I guess the Convent is my child.

> *(She leaves. A terrible silence. **PATTI** breathing heavily, **JILL** not breathing at all.)*

JILL. Patti.

PATTI. Fuck off, Jill. Go back to your husband.

> *(**JILL** watches **PATTI** start pacing around, like an animal.)*

JILL. Patti –

PATTI. I said FUCK OFF.

> *(A tense beat. **JILL** leaves.)*
>
> *(**PATTI** stops, crying, rips at her skin for a moment, tears at herself in some way.)*
>
> *(So much pain.)*

I want to be a good fucking person.
I want to stop pretending I'm *not a* good person.
I want to have power in my hands.
I want to heal things with my touch.
I want to start with myself.
I want the truth, even when it's hard.
I want love. The real fuckin' thing.
I want to wipe all the shitty graffiti scrawled all over my heart – clear it off so I can see what's really there.
What it's really made of.
I want a home.
A place where I can close my eyes.
And dream.
And change.
Amen.

11.

> *(Everyone at dinner. **PATTI** is missing. **MOTHER ABBESS** stares darkly toward the empty chair. Everyone waits. After a beat, because **TINA** is so fucking wonderful, she stands.)*

TINA. I'd like to make an announcement:
I've been sneaking out at night?
And there is a really nice man in his fifties
or he might actually be in his late seventies
but the point is he is really generous.
He gave me some pot on like my first day here
and I've been sort of "trading" with him ever since...
The point is his roommates are this really beautiful old lesbian couple who have been together since they were like my age and I was really baked and they told me that lubricant basically saved their marriage.
It's like apparently God's gift to womankind and I just thought I would pass that to you all.

ALL. ...

TINA. *(Particularly to **DIMLIN** and **BERTIE**.)* They call it Lubrifeunt here.
In case anyone wants to BUY SOME.
The French are so amazing. They eat bread all day, they embrace that life is complicated, and they call the vagina a Shoopinette. They have so much to teach us.

MOTHER ABBESS. *(After a disturbed beat.)* Thank you, Tina.

TINA. You're welcome.

> *(She sits.)*

> *(An uncomfortable beat while the group gauges **MOTHER ABBESS**.)*

JILL. *(A little to **MOTHER ABBESS**, but also to the table in general.)* Does anyone know anything about Teresa of Ávila?

> *(Will **MOTHER ABBESS** respond?)*

I admit I haven't been very *attentive* here and I'm trying…

> *(A beat to see if* **MOTHER ABBESS** *will respond. She is now deeply meditating on the empty chair. So* **WILMA** *helps:)*

WILMA. Teresa of Ávila.

JILL. Yeah.

WILMA. She's a good one.

JILL. I'm fucked, right? She was like an Uber Mystic, right?

WILMA. She was. She was an Uber Mystic.

JILL. Yeah. I'm fucked.

WILMA. Saint Teresa said,
"Let nothing upset you.
Let nothing frighten you.
Everything is changing.
God alone is changeless.
Patience attains the goal.
Who has God lacks nothing.
God alone fills all her needs."

JILL. *Her* needs? She wrote that?

WILMA. She did. It makes a difference, doesn't it? Hearing your pronoun. She wrote a book called *The Interior Castle*.

JILL. *The Interior Castle.*

WILMA. The title alone sends your imagination in the right direction, doesn't it?

> *(Another beat while everyone wonders how to proceed.)*

MOTHER ABBESS. We can't wait any longer. Go ahead and begin, Wilma.

> *(So* **WILMA** *stands. Sensitive to Patti's empty chair, she gently begins:)*

WILMA. My name is Hildegard von Bingen.
I lived in Germany in the mid-1100s.

All my life I knew God, had visions of God.
I studied plants and herbal medicine.
I wrote volumes of books.
I believed music could heal.
I wrote very colorfully about the male erection.
Actually this is worth going into – I theorized that the penis had two small tents of fire on either side, and this is what caused it to *rise*... I know, right?
(Maybe gently aimed to **DIMLIN.***)* I had an intense, complicated relationship with a young nun who helped me – she helped me run the convent, she helped me write my books – she was devoted. For a time. But I lost her.
Whipping oneself, starving for Christ, this was very common back then, but not in my convent.
When a nun in my charge was doing this I would say:

> *(She speaks to each of the women. At some point,* **MOTHER ABBESS** *looks up and listens.)*

"Why do you hurt yourself?
I am your Mother and I say to you, 'Do not rip your beautiful body.
Think of your body as a little girl in your care.
She cannot fix your suffering, nor does she cause it.
Do not ask her to suffer.
Do not raise your hand against her.
Do not cut yourself.
Do not hit yourself.
Do not starve yourself.
Do not shame your heart.
Do not punish your life.
Do not hurt yourself.
Do not hurt yourself.
Do not hurt yourself.'"

> *(She sits.)*

MOTHER ABBESS. *(Heavy-hearted.)* Thank you, Wilma.

(Beat.)

WILMA. Let us pray.

(Everyone bows their head.)

...

...

...

God...?

*(She begins to sing a song from that same major female pop artist [that Tina sang in the garden]. In its original form the song should feel sexy, feminist, and fun, but as **WILMA** sings it now, it is slower, more gentle, reverent, almost holy. Eventually everyone [except **MOTHER ABBESS**] has joined in. It should feel like a prayer.*)*

(Immediately into –)

---

*A license to produce *The Convent* does not include a performance license for any third-party or copyrighted music. Licensees should create an original composition or use music in the public domain. For further information, please see Music Use Note on page 3.

12.

(Late in the night. **MOTHER ABBESS** *goes to Patti's room, watches her. But* **PATTI** *is not asleep. From the dark:)*

MOTHER ABBESS. Can I come in?
You used to do this. When you were little. Come into our room and stand at the bed right by my face. I knew the second I moved you'd want to crawl into bed with me, so I'd stay frozen so you'd think I was asleep and go back to your room.

(They sit like that for a moment.)

I'm ill, Patti.
Ovarian cancer.
I'm aware of the irony.
The things that are inside you and you don't even know it.
'Til you do.

(Beat.)

PATTI. I have this memory.
I don't know how old I am – maybe two? Three?
Remember that ugly bathtub in Providence?
With all the ugly orange tiles?

MOTHER ABBESS. They were more like – blood – orange. Ish.

PATTI. Exactly.
...
We were in that bathtub.
There were candles on the sink.
All the little toothbrushes were sort of twinkling.
And there might've been singing? Not sure.
I was sitting between your legs in the tub, playing with a cup...
You were leaning against the back of the tub.

I could see your collarbone, your neck, gleaming with beads of sweat and water.

Your breasts would float up and peek above the water, and then back under.

Your eyelashes were wet and heavy.

But you were watching me.

With this soft smile.

And I knew.

I knew you loved me.

(Tears roll down **MOTHER ABBESS**'*face. Looking into her daughter's eyes:)*

MOTHER ABBESS. What is it you really want, Patti?

PATTI. *(Simply, beautifully.)* You. I want you.

MOTHER ABBESS. *(Very quietly.)* Patti.

PATTI. *(So, so quietly.)* Momma.

(They are both crying.)

MOTHER ABBESS. Please.

Please.

Please.

Let me go.

(A terrible silence. Blackout.)

13.

> (**BERTIE**, **PATTI**, **JILL**, **WILMA**, *and* **TINA** *are gathered.)*
>
> (**MOTHER ABBESS** *is not there. Nor is* **DIMLIN**.)
>
> *(After a moment:)*

JILL. Has anyone seen her? Has anyone seen Mother Abbess?

> *(No one has.)*

Where's Dimlin? She's the Number Two.

> *(Everyone looks to* **BERTIE**.*)*

BERTIE. *(Quietly.)* I haven't seen her.

> *(Beat.)*

JILL. What should we do?

> *(Beat.)*

PATTI. *(Exhausted, broken open, but sincere.)* Usually on the final day she says something wrappy-uppy...like...

> *(But then it happens. Just like that.* **PATTI** *is like the new* **MOTHER ABBESS**.*)*

You came to the Convent
because you felt spiritually bankrupt.
You chose your Nomen.
And now your time here has come to an end.
You will return your robe.
Your Nomen is yours to keep.
So if there's anything you wanna say – That's now.

WILMA. I thought if I could go back in time there would be less noise.
There would only be well water, stones, my growling stomach.
And down in those ancient, barren sounds, I would hear God again.

Or whatever it is that mystics and physicists and poets
and schizophrenics have been hearing for millennia.
But maybe I stopped hearing for a reason.
Maybe it's time to go find *people*.
Or one particular person.
The world has a lot to offer.
I just want to thank you all.

    *(She sits. **TINA** rises.)*

TINA. I came because I wanted every moment in my life to
be a Renaissance faire.
I like candlelight.
And men in armor.
I really really like men in armor.
A lot.
Big time.
But I guess now I think I came because
I miss my mom.
But maybe the world *is* a mom.
Maybe the whole world is one big beautiful mom.

    *(She sits. **BERTIE** rises.)*

BERTIE. I came to the Convent...because Dimlin brought
me.
And I want to go wherever Dimlin is.
Cora Elizabeth Wellington Dimlin.
I've never been much.
But with Dimlin, I'm just right.
I'm the other part of whatever is not her.
And I thought – I thought there would always be
Dimlin.
And if there is not? – ... If there is not Dimlin...?
Then –

    (The door suddenly slams open – there stands
    DIMLIN. *She is extraordinarily out of breath.*
    She is holding a big bottle of lube.)

DIMLIN. *(Trying to breathe.)* Wait! Wait.
(*Lungs burning.*) I want to say that...
(*Dying of no air.*) Fuck me those stairs.
(*Holding her side stitch.*) I want to say that...I love you
Bertie.

BERTIE. You –?

DIMLIN. Love you. I love you.

BERTIE. You do?

DIMLIN. I love you.

BERTIE. Oh Dimlin.

DIMLIN. I do.

BERTIE. Yes.

DIMLIN. I love you.

BERTIE. Yes.

DIMLIN. *(A plane ticket.)* This is for you.

BERTIE. Oh Dimlin.

DIMLIN. A ticket to Gloucestershire.

BERTIE. Dimlin!

DIMLIN. To meet my bloody family.

BERTIE. *(Crying with happiness now.)* Yes!

DIMLIN. And this.

BERTIE. And what?

DIMLIN. This!

> (*She thrusts the lubricant – i.e. Lubrifeunt –
> clutched in her sweaty hand at* **BERTIE.***)*

BERTIE. LUBRIFEUNT!

TINA. YYYEEEEESSSSSSSSS!!!!

DIMLIN. You know about Lubrifeunt?

TINA. I told her too! All good!

DIMLIN. I love you.

BERTIE. I love you.

DIMLIN. I love you.

BERTIE. I love you.

(They disappear into kisses. It's wonderful, like two old twin sisters who are lovers [haha]. Then they see everyone else. The women clap for them. They curtsy.)

DIMLIN. Well that was quite a show.

BERTIE. Wasn't it?

DIMLIN. Quite the matinee.

BERTIE. Indeed.

DIMLIN. That'll be forty quid.

BERTIE. Oh naughty!

DIMLIN. Quite naughty.

BERTIE. Quite quite.

(And they kiss again, intimate, snuggled, they sit down.)

*(And then in walks **MOTHER ABBESS**. She looks like absolute hell. She holds the chalice.)*

MOTHER ABBESS. Sorry I'm late.

(Everyone just looks at her.)

I'd never done it.
The Head of Kings?
I'd never done it.
It's terrifying.
There's no other word for it.
Terrifying.
And devastating.

JILL. What did you see? In the Head of Kings.

(Beat.)

MOTHER ABBESS. Me. My King – was me.

*(No one knows what to say. **MOTHER ABBESS** looks to **PATTI**.)*

PATTI. I came to the Convent
to be with my mother.
To punish her, possess her, destroy her.

But now?
I don't know.
I don't know what now.

(Beat. Then **JILL** *stands.)*

JILL. My name is Teresa of Ávila.
I wrote a book called *The Interior Castle*.
I think – I pretended to write to my sisters, the nuns in my care,
but really, I was writing to myself.
With the kind of counsel I desperately needed.
And somehow, through this call and response within myself –
I *built an* Interior Castle.
A gleaming tower with walls and turrets all made of glass.
And in this great castle I can see something shimmering.
So I wander the rooms, trying to find this light source –
I see it reflected everywhere – this light –
sparkling in the glass tables and chairs, the glass ceiling and floor.
I intend to keep seeking until I find it
and eventually, I will attain the goal:
I will *become* Teresa of Ávila.

MOTHER ABBESS. Or Jill.

JILL. Or Jill.

MOTHER ABBESS. Or Wilma.
Or Dimlin and Bertie.
Or Tina.
Or Patti.
May *we all* become one worthy of such a castle.

14.
The Epilogue

(About three weeks later. **PATTI***, a little drunk, waits for the F train at Second Ave, or somewhere equally depressing. She sways a little as she lights a cigarette.)*

PATTI. *(On phone.)* Hey, it's Patti. Where are you right now, you wanna meet up?

(Sucking hard on that cig.)

Oh. That's cool.

Yeah, France was uhhh...

Actually, I was –

I was supposed to go back – to spend some time with her, or –

But... She died. My mom. She died tonight...

You sure you can't meet me?

Oh. No I get it. Yeah I'll be fine.

I mean, I hardly knew her, right? ...

Sure yeah bye...

(She shuts the phone, hands immediately to her face.)

(A **HOMELESS WOMAN***, hair crazy, dirty, reeking of mental illness, shouts at her from across the platform:)*

HOMELESS WOMAN. HHHAAAAGHH Got a dollar?

PATTI. Uh – *(Gauging the distance.)* – Sorry.

(The **HOMELESS WOMAN** *stares at her, unsteady on her feet.)*

HOMELESS WOMAN. You're a twat.

PATTI. I'm –?

HOMELESS WOMAN. Twat you're a twat. You're twattish. When you make love, it's all –

(She strikes a fakey sex pose.)

PATTI. Okay.

HOMELESS WOMAN. It's like –

> *(She strikes another fakey sex pose, loud, even violent.)*

PATTI. I'm ignoring you.

> *(The* **HOMELESS WOMAN** *strikes another fakey sex pose, even more loud and violent.)*

PATTI. *(Frayed, unraveling.)* I'm not in a good place at the moment, so you might wanna –

> *(The* **HOMELESS WOMAN***'s mocking of* **PATTI** *turns into a mental illness spasm, slapping herself, spitting sex sounds and bizarre animal sounds. It's scary.)*

Okay fuck you fuck you and your mental illness. Crazy fuckin' –

> *(The* **HOMELESS WOMAN** *keeps going with the insanity.)*

(Suddenly broken, weeping, done.) Goddammit you have no idea how fragile I am right now.

HOMELESS WOMAN. *(Suddenly clear and fierce, like a powerful force is coming through her body.)* Your job is to love your life.
YOUR JOB
Is to LOVE
YOUR
LIFE.

> *(***PATTI** *is suddenly listening.)*

Not your work,
Not your family,
Not your habits,
Not your coffee,
Not your clothes,
Not your friends or your rugs or your history or your plans

Not even your faith
Not even your truths
But your Life.
That fierce
Hungry
Flame
Inside you –
That feral fucking thing
Right in here
That says,

> *(Like a heartbeat.)*

"NOW
NOW
NOW."
That
is your life.
If you can love that
you will always do the right thing.

> *(They stare at one another. Panting. A moment of tense nothingness, no one moves. Then, quietly, maybe testing it:)*

PATTI. Now.
Now.
Now.

> *(She slowly smiles. Realizes what has happened, what is happening. The* **HOMELESS WOMAN** *smiles too. Then suddenly, together:)*

PATTI & HOMELESS WOMAN. HHHAAAAGHHH!!!!

> *(Blackout.)*

End of Play